Skip to My Lou

Skip to My Lou

adapted and illustrated by
Nadine Bernard Westcott

Joy Street Books
Little, Brown and Company
Boston Toronto London

To my mother and father

First edition

Library of Congress Cataloging-in-Publication Data

Westcott, Nadine Bernard.
    Skip to my Lou / by Nadine Bernard Westcott. — 1st ed.
        p.   cm.
    Summary: When his parents leave a young boy in charge of the farm
for a day, chaos erupts as the animals take over the house.
    ISBN 0-316-93137-3
    [1. Farm life — Fiction. 2. Humorous stories. 3. Stories in
rhyme.] I. Title.
PZ8.3.W4998Sk   1989
[E] — dc19   88-7306
                                                       CIP
                                                        AC

10 9 8 7 6 5 4 3 2 1

Joy Street Books are published by
Little, Brown and Company (Inc.)

Published simultaneously in Canada
by Little, Brown & Company (Canada) Limited

WOR

Printed in the United States of America

Skip to My Lou

Chorus

Lou,   Lou,   skip   to   my   Lou,   Lou,   Lou,   skip   to   my   Lou,

Lou,   Lou,   skip   to   my   Lou,   Skip   to   my   Lou,   my   dar - ling!

Musical notation of "Skip to My Lou" from *Singing Bee!* by Jane Hart. Musical arrangement Copyright © 1982 by Jane Hart. By permission of Lothrop, Lee & Shepard (A Division of William Morrow & Co., Inc.).

Sitting on the front porch,
Painted like new —
The farm's all in order,
There's not much to do.

"Take care of the farm.
We'll be back by two!"

Skip to my Lou, my darling!

Flies in the sugarbowl,

Shoo fly shoo.

Cats in the buttermilk,

Two by two.

Pigs in the parlor,
What'll I do?

Skip to my Lou, my darling!

Cows in the kitchen,
Moo cow moo.

Roosters in the pantry,

Cock-a-doodle-do.

Sheep in the bathtub,

Hulla-baloo!

Skip to my Lou, my darling!

Lou, Lou, skip to my Lou,
Lou, Lou, skip to my Lou,

Lou, Lou, skip to my Lou,
Skip to my Lou, my darling!

Look at the clock,
It's a quarter to two!
Goodness gracious,
What will we do?

Hurry, quick! It's up to you!

Skip to my Lou, my darling!

Phew!